Snow White

Picture Window Books
Minneapolis, Minnesota

First published in the United States in 2010
by Picture Window Books
A Capstone Imprint
151 Good Counsel Drive
P.O. Box 669
Mankato, Minnesota 56002
www.capstonepub.com

©2005, Edizioni El S.r.l., Treiste Italy in BIANCANEVE

Printed in the United States of America in North Mankato, Minnesota.
032010
005718R

All books published by Picture Window Books
are manufactured with paper containing
at least 10 percent post-consumer waste.

Library of Congress Cataloging-in-Publication Data
Piumini, Roberto.
[Biancaneve. English] Snow White / by Roberto Piumini ; illustrated by Anna Laura Cantone.
p. cm. — (Storybook classics)
ISBN 978-1-4048-5644-8 (library binding)
[1. Fairy tales. 2. Folklore—Germany.] I. Cantone, Anna Laura, ill. II. Snow White and the seven
dwarfs. English. III. Title.
PZ8.P717Sn 2010
398.2—dc22
[E]   2009010461

Snow White

Retold by Roberto Piumini

Illustrated by Anna Laura Cantone

Once upon a time, a king had a daughter named Snow White. Their life together was happy, but he missed his wife, who had died years before. So one day, he decided to marry another woman, who was very beautiful.

Every evening, the new queen, who was secretly an evil witch, asked her mirror, "Mirror, mirror on the wall, who is the fairest of them all?"

The mirror always replied, "I give the same answer each time you call — *you* are the fairest of them all."

ut one evening, the mirror's reply was different.

"You are beautiful, my queen, it's true. But Snow White, your stepdaughter, is now fairer than you," it replied.

The witch screamed at the mirror in anger. She went to a hunter and told him, "Take Snow White into the woods and kill her!"

The hunter did as he was told and took Snow White into the woods. But he did not have the heart to kill her, for she was so sweet and lovely.

"Run far away, Snow White," he told her. "Your life is in danger."

So she ran.

Snow White ran deeper and deeper into the woods. Soon she became cold and hungry and afraid. Suddenly, she saw a little house in the forest with light in its windows. Cheerful voices came from inside.

Snow White walked up to the house and knocked. When the door opened, she saw seven dwarves smiling at her.

"What are you doing outside on this cold, dark night?" they asked. "Come inside!"

So Snow White stayed with the seven dwarves in their little house.

Every day, the little men went off to work in the mine. By the time they came home, Snow White had cleaned the house, made the beds, and prepared dinner. She even made them little cakes, which the dwarves loved.

Their life was quiet and peaceful, and it seemed that they would be happy forever.

Back at the castle, the evil queen once again questioned her mirror, "Mirror, mirror on the wall, who is the fairest of them all?"

"You are as fair as fair may be, but between you and Snow White, the fairer is she," replied the mirror.

Furious, the witch ground her teeth and clenched her fists. She confronted the hunter. He had no choice but to tell her the truth: he had let Snow White escape.

The queen was determined to kill Snow White. She went into the woods herself and searched for the young girl. Soon she spotted a house in the distance. Snow White was hanging the laundry out to dry.

Disguised as an old woman, the witch knocked on the door of the little house.

"How can I help you, good lady?" asked Snow White.

"Would you like to buy one of my delicious apples?" asked the old woman.

Snow White looked at the apples. She thought that they would make a tasty pie for the dwarves.

"Taste this one, my dear!" said the old woman, showing her the largest, most colorful apple.

Snow White took one bite and fell to the ground.

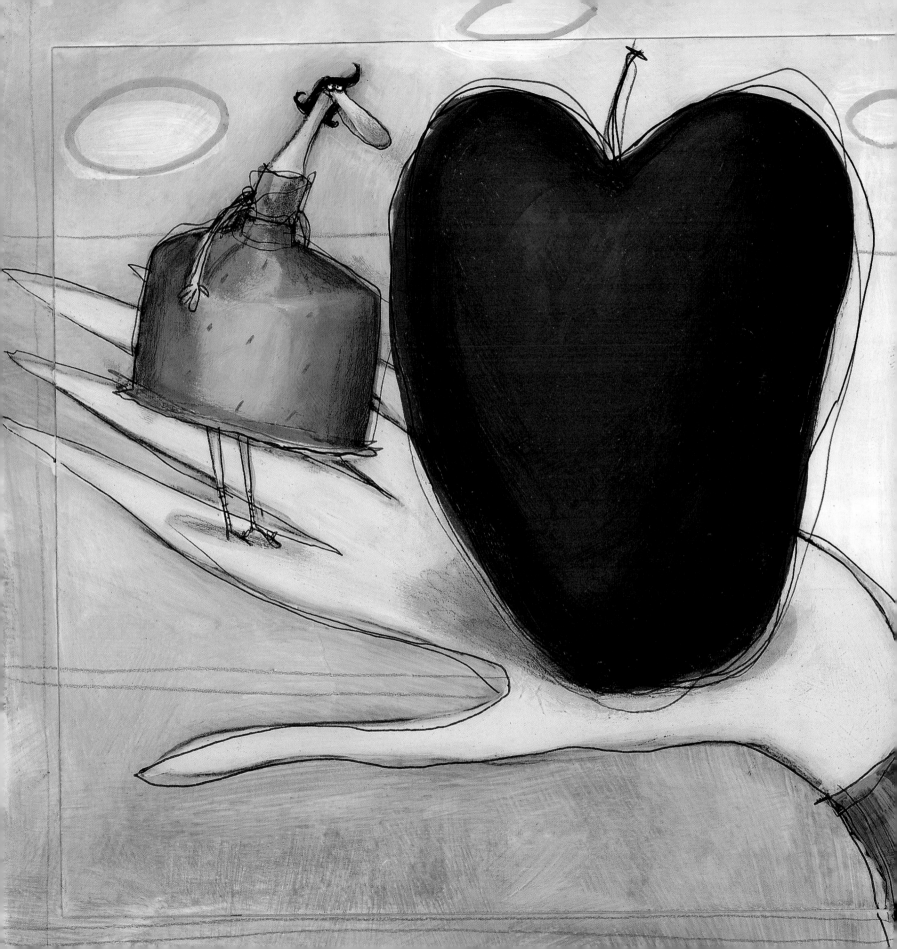

When the dwarves returned home from the mine, they found that Snow White had been poisoned.

After crying for hours, the dwarves built a glass casket for Snow White and placed her in it. They carried the casket to the top of a mountain where flowers grew and guarded it day and night.

One day, a prince came by. He saw Snow White lying in her glass casket and instantly fell in love.

"Let me take her to the palace," he said to the dwarves. "I'll put a thousand fresh flowers around her casket every day, and my guards will watch over her day and night."

He begged and begged until the dwarves said yes.

The prince had his servants place the glass casket on top of his carriage. They took it to the castle, with the prince riding his horse behind them to make sure Snow White was safe.

"Slow down, or the casket will fall!" he said.

When they reached the entrance of the prince's palace, one of the carriage wheels hit a large tree root that stuck up from the road. The casket fell off the carriage, and Snow White tumbled out. The fall shook loose a piece of poisoned apple that had been stuck in her throat.

Suddenly, Snow White opened her eyes.

"Where am I?" she asked the prince. "Who are you?"

The prince was full of joy. He explained everything that had happened to Snow White.

"Now I remember," she said. "An old woman came and gave me the apple. Who was she?"

"I'm afraid no one knows. But I have a question for you, Snow White," the prince said as he dropped to one knee. "Will you be my wife?"

"Yes," Snow White replied with a smile.

The entire kingdom was invited to the wedding, including Snow White's stepmother, the evil queen.

When she saw Snow White alive and dressed in a bride's gown, she turned bright red with anger.

"I should have put more poison in that apple!" she shouted.

The prince heard the queen's outburst, and he ordered his guards to arrest her. Two iron shoes were heated in a fire, and the witch was forced to wear them. She ran away howling and was never seen again.

Snow White and the prince went on to have seven children — three beautiful girls and four brave boys.

Snow White often took her children to the small house in the woods to visit the dwarves.

The little men were the perfect playmates. And the children loved being in a place where everything was the perfect size.

FAIRY TALE
Follow-Up

1. Why did the evil stepmother want Snow White killed?

2. After Snow White moves in with the dwarves, she makes a routine of cooking and cleaning every day. The story says, "It seemed that they would be happy forever." Did you think their life would indeed be "happy forever"?

3. Have you heard another version of Snow White? Was the ending different? Were there other differences?

4. What was your favorite part of the story? Why?

Glossary

clenched (KLENCHT)—held or squeezed something tightly

confronted (kuhn-FRUHNT-id)—met or faced someone in a threatening way

disguised (diss-GIZED)—dressed in a way that hides who someone really is

furious (FYU-ree-uhss)—very angry

instantly (IN-stuhnt-lee)—right away

outburst (OUT-burst)—a sudden pouring out of emotions

WRITE YOUR OWN
Fairy Tale

Fairy tales have been told for hundreds of years. Most fairy tales share certain elements, or pieces. Once you learn about these elements, you can try writing your own fairy tales.

Element 1: The Characters

Characters are the people, animals, or other creatures in the story. They can be good or evil, silly or serious. Can you name the characters in *Snow White*? There are Snow White, the evil queen, the mirror, the hunter, the seven dwarves, and the prince.

Element 2: The Setting

The setting tells us *when* and *where* a story takes place. The *when* of the story could be a hundred years ago or a hundred years in the future. There may be more than one *where* in a story. You could go from a house to a school to a park. In *Snow White*, the story says it happened "once upon a time." Usually this means that it takes place many years ago. And *where* does it take place? It begins in Snow White's palace, then heads to the woods and the dwarves' home, before finishing in the prince's castle.

Element 3: The Plot

Think about what happens in the story. You are thinking about the plot, or the action of the story. In fairy tales, the action begins nearly right away. In *Snow White*, the plot begins on the first page. The stepmother asks her mirror, "Mirror, mirror on the wall, who is the fairest of them all?" And the story takes off from there!

Element 4: Magic

Did you know that all fairy tales have an element of magic? The magic is what makes a fairy tale different from other stories. Often, the magic comes in the form of a character that doesn't exist in real life, such as a giant, a witch, or in the case of *Snow White*, a talking mirror. What other magic is there in Snow White?

Element 5: A Happy Ending

Years ago, fairy tales ended on a sad note, but today, most fairy tales have a happy ending. Readers like knowing that the hero of the story has beaten the villain. Did *Snow White* have a happy ending? Of course! Snow White married her prince, and the evil queen met her punishment.

Now that you know the basic elements of a fairy tale, try writing your own! Create characters, both good and bad. Decide when and where their story will take place to give them a setting. Now put them into action during the plot of the story. Don't forget that you need some magic! And finally, give the hero of your story a happy ending.

ABOUT THE
Author

Roberto Piumini lives and works in Italy. He has worked with children as both a teacher and a theater actor/entertainer. He credits these experiences for inspiring the youthful language of his many books. With his crisp and imaginative way of dealing with every kind of subject, he keeps charming his young readers. His award-winning books, for both children and adults, have been translated into many languages.

ABOUT THE
Illustrator

Anna Laura Cantone holds a degree in illustration for children's books from the European Design Institution in Milan. Several of her works have been translated into other languages. She is the recipient of several awards, including the Andersen Award at the Bologna children's book fair. In addition to book illustrations, her work has appeared in specialty magazines. When she's not illustrating, she exhibits her sculptures, paintings, and installations.

More Tales to Treasure

Open a Storybook Classic and experience the world of traditional fairy tales told through simple prose and splendid artwork. These safe and inventive picture books feature beautiful and whimsical illustrations that will charm young and old alike.

STORYBOOK Classics
THE 3 LITTLE PIGS
Retold by Roberta Pineiro
Illustrated by Nicoletta Ceccoli

STORYBOOK Classics
Cinderella
Retold by Roberta Pineiro
Illustrated by Raffaella Ligi

STORYBOOK Classics
Hansel and Gretel
Retold by Roberta Pineiro
Illustrated by Anna Laura Cantone

STORYBOOK Classics
GOLDILOCKS and the Three Bears
retold by Roberta Pineiro
illustrated by Valentina Salmaso

STORYBOOK Classics
Pinocchio
retold by Roberta Pineiro
Illustrated by Lucia Salemi

STORYBOOK Classics
Puss in Boots

STORYBOOK Classics
little RED RIDING HOOD